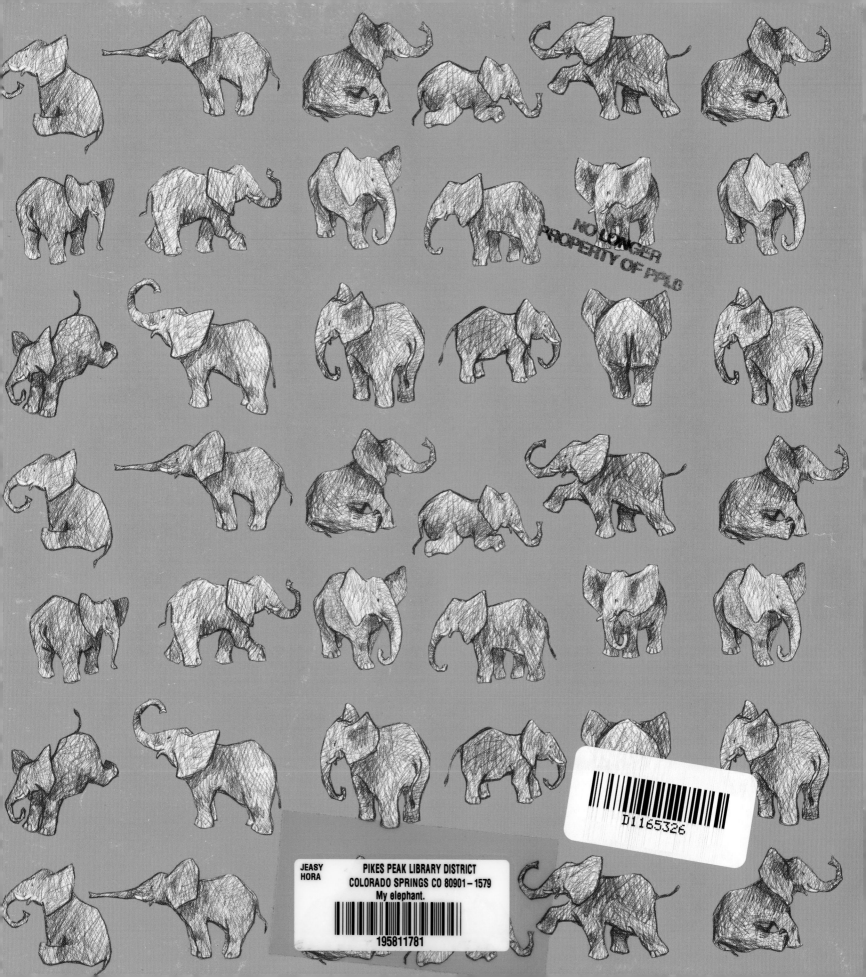

To Marin, Vincent, and Max

MY
E LEP

First U.S. edition 2009.
Library of Congress Cataloging-in-Publication Data is available. Library of Congress Catalog Card Number 2008940804. ISBN 978-0-7636-4566-3. 09 10 11 12 13 SCP 10 9 8 7 6 5 4 3 2
Printed in Humen, Dongguan, China. This book was typeset in Horáček. The illustrations were done in mixed med
Candlewick Press, 99 Dover Street, Somerville, Massachusetts 02144
visit us at www.candlewick.com

Petr Horáček

ELEPHANT

CANDLEWICK PRESS

I asked Grandpa to play ball
with me, but he was too busy.

I went to
see Grandma,
but she was
busy, too.

So I asked my **ELEPHANT** if *he* wanted to play with me.

We played kickball
in the yard.

Then Grandpa called out, "Who MESSED UP the flower bed?"

"I'm sorry, Grandpa," I said.

"It was my ELEPHANT."

Grandpa didn't believe me,
so I took my ELEPHANT inside.

Then Grandma called out,
"Who MESSED UP the hallway?"

"I'm sorry, Grandma," I said.

"It must have been
my ELEPHANT."

"And was it your ELEPHANT who SPLASHED and made puddles in the bathroom?" she asked.

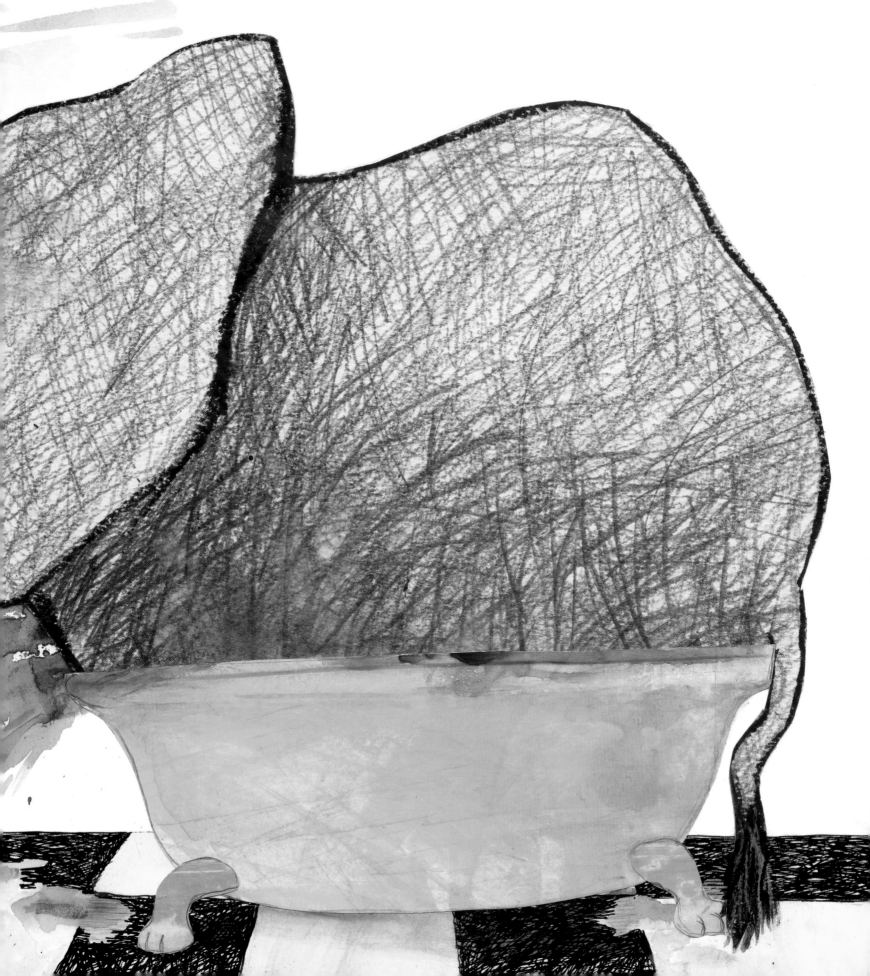

"And was it your ELEPHANT who KNOCKED OVER the orange juice?" she asked.

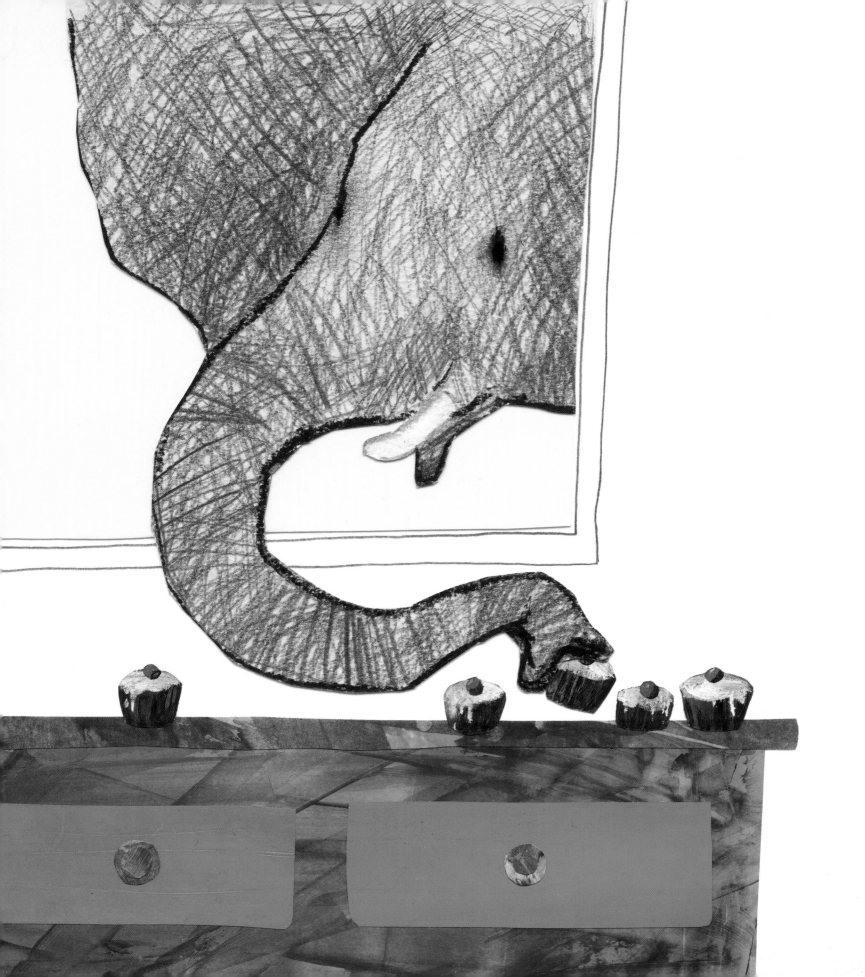

"And was it your ELEPHANT who ATE the cupcakes?" Grandma asked.

"Well, yes," I replied.

Grandma looked at me as if she didn't believe me.

That made me sad.

I wanted

to be

alone.

Then my ELEPHANT
came over. He smiled
at me. I said that
I was sorry for
telling on him.

Then I
felt better.

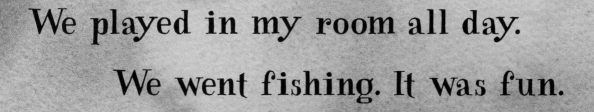

We played in my room all day.
We went fishing. It was fun.

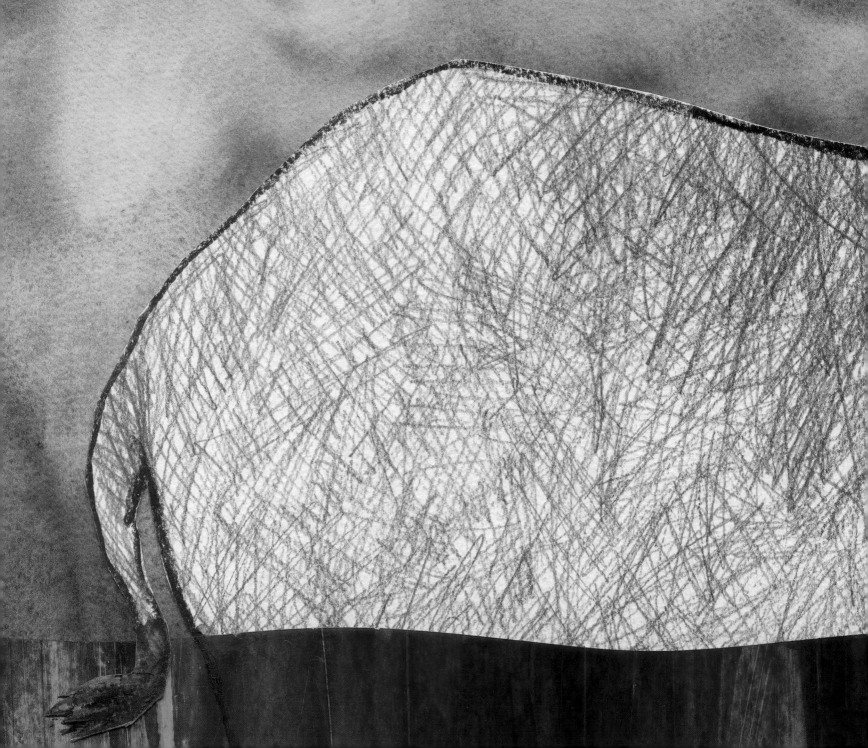

Then my ELEPHANT took me to
the jungle to see tigers. Soon . . .

it was morning! Grandpa wanted to play ball.

"But how did I end up
here?" I asked.

"You were tired,"
Grandpa said.

"So your ELEPHANT
carried you to bed!"

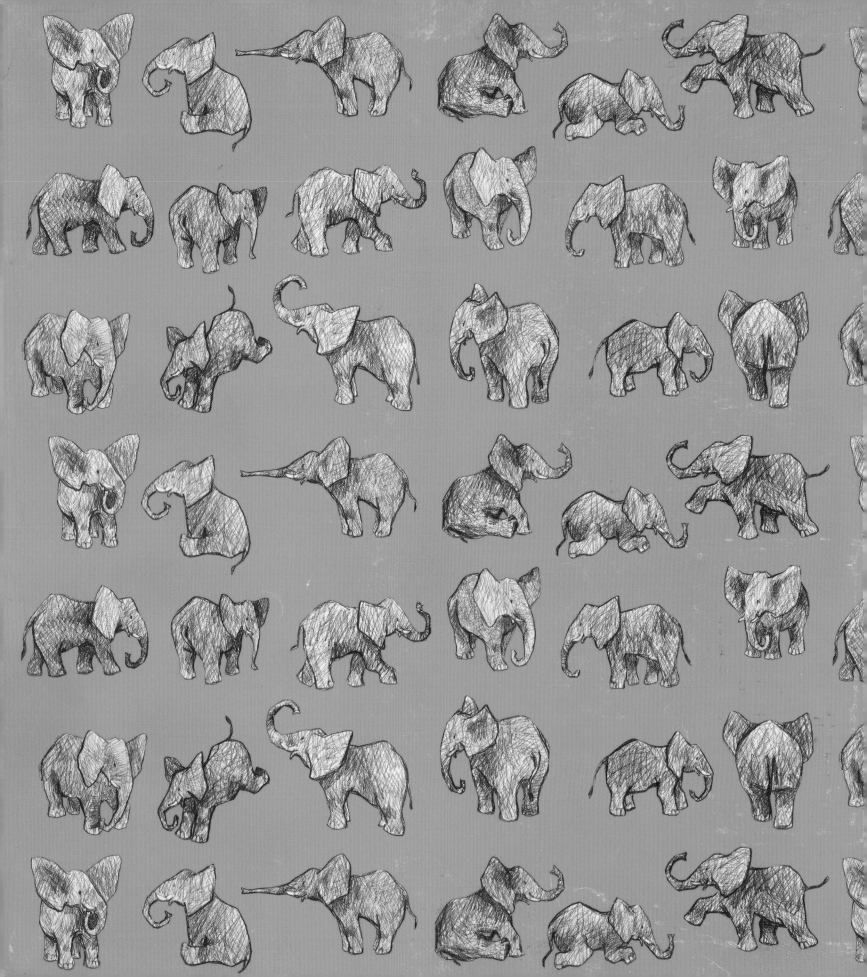